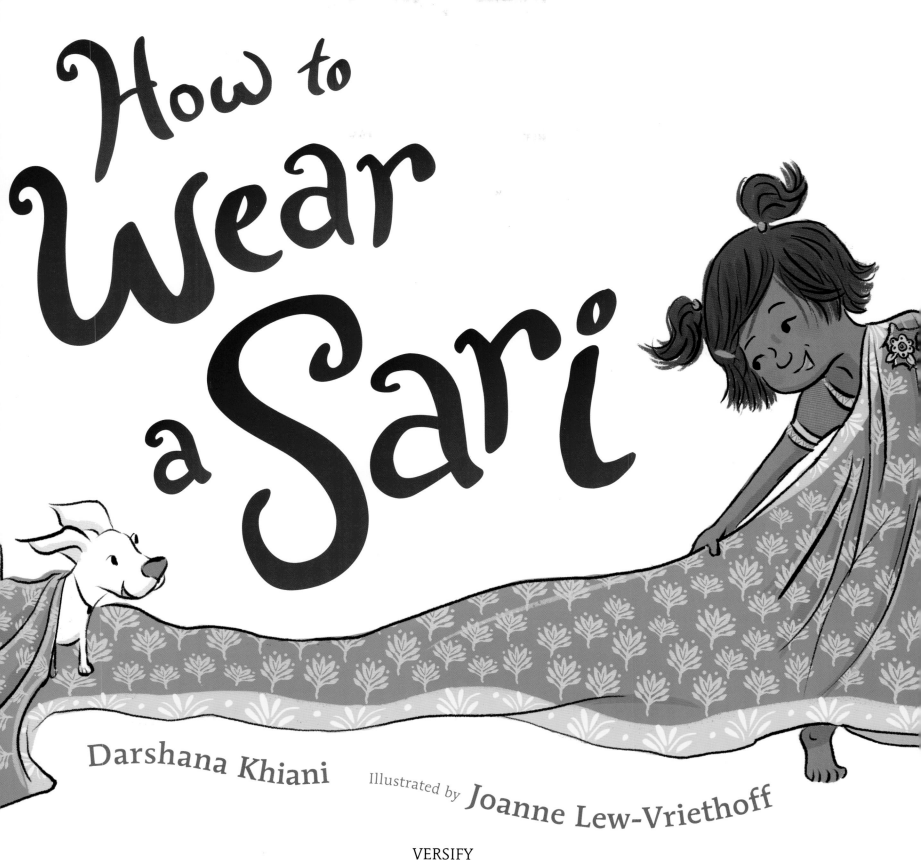

How to Wear a Sari

Darshana Khiani

Illustrated by Joanne Lew-Vriethoff

VERSIFY

HOUGHTON MIFFLIN HARCOURT

BOSTON   NEW YORK

Are you tired of being treated like a little kid?

"You're too small."

"That's too difficult."

"Aww, how cute."

Do you want to show them you
can do grown-up things too?
All you need is a . . .

colorful, twinkly, silky sari.

Don't be nervous.
Sure, saris are long and unwieldy and worn by adults, but you can do it.

Your family will definitely take notice.

You'll be a **pro.**

They'll stop to take **photos**, consult you for tips, and maybe even give you a **contract**.

First, you need to find the **perfect** sari.

It can be tricky when there are so many **choices.**

Too plain.

Too fancy.

Needs more sparkle.

Don't know where else to **look?**

Ask your friend for help.

She'll know where to **search.**

Gorgeous choice!

You'll look so grown-up wearing it.
Your family will be amazed.

Let's get **started**.

Take one end of the sari and start **tucking it in**.

Hmm . . .
something's missing.

Put the sari blouse and petticoat on first.

A little **long**.

Make some adjustments.

And they said you were too small. Silly adults.

Now tuck and spin.

Are you okay? Can you **breathe?**

Unwrap and try again. This time a little **looser.**

Next, the hardest part—the PLEATS.

If you can master this, your mom will be so impressed.
Hold the sari and fold it back and forth, back and forth . . .

Try not to **drop** any.

It's okay to get **help**.

Let's check out the **pleats**.

Too **small**. Try again.

Too **big**. One more time.

Suck your belly in and **tuck**.

Good job!

Nothing is too difficult for you. You're a **pro!**
Aunties will be asking you for **tips.**

You're **almost** done.
Toss the extra sari over your shoulder
and pin it to your **blouse**.

Don't worry . . .

a dazzling **brooch** can cover up any hole.

Love the jewelry!

Now find some **sparkly** sandals.
No sari is complete without them.

Magnificent!

Go show them your **glamorous grown-up** look.

Remember not to run.

Well, you got your picture taken,

a consultation,

and even a contract.

I will not
when in moms

Look on the **bright side**—you've achieved a **family milestone**.

You now have a spot in the **Hall of Fame** album along with the rest of them.

Text copyright © 2021 by Darshana Khiani
Illustrations copyright © 2021 by Joanne Lew-Vriethoff

Versify® is an imprint of Houghton Mifflin Harcourt Publishing Company.
Versify is a registered trademark of Houghton Mifflin Harcourt Publishing Company.

hmhbooks.com

The illustrations in this book were digitally drawn and colored.
The text type was set in ITC Mendoza.
Design by Natalie Fondriest

Library of Congress Cataloging-in-Publication Data
Names: Khiani, Darshana, author. | Lew-Vriethoff, Joanne, illustrator.
Title: How to wear a sari / Darshana Khiani ; illustrated by Joanne Lew-Vriethoff.
Description: Boston : Houghton Mifflin Harcourt, [2021] | Audience: Ages 4 to 7. | Audience: Grades K–1. | Summary: Tired of being treated like a child, a young girl sets out to prove herself capable to her multi-generational Indian-American family, but an ill-fated attempt at putting on a sari has an unexpected outcome.
Identifiers: LCCN 2019036683 | ISBN 9781328635204 (hardcover)
Subjects: CYAC: Youngest child—Fiction. | Family life—Fiction. | Saris—Fiction. | East Indian Americans—Fiction.
Classification: LCC PZ7.1.K534 How 2021 | DDC [E]—dc23
LC record available at https://lccn.loc.gov/2019036683

Manufactured in China
SCP 10 9 8 7 6 5 4 3 2 1
4500820222